FRIGHTFUL FAMILIES

POPSTAR PANIC

SUE MONGREDIEN • TERESA MURFIN

ORCHARD BOOKS

Bee-Bee Bell was a pop sensation. She had crooned for kings and queens. She had performed for presidents and prime ministers, and she had sung at sell-out tours all over the world. She was also Jessica's mum.

Once upon a time, Jessica had thought it was pretty cool to be a popstar's daughter. After all, not every baby had had lullabies sung to them by celebrities. Jessica had.

Not every toddler had played the tambourine in concert stadiums around the world. Jessica had.

And there weren't many children who could dance in high heels at the age of four. Jessica could.

But by the time Jessica was at school, she had started to wonder if being a popstar's daughter was such a great thing after all.

The girls at Jessica's school thought she was really lucky to have a famous mum. And sometimes, it was brilliant. Jessica certainly didn't complain about having ponies, exotic holidays or a personal stylist.

But sometimes, Jessica wished her mum was more like everyone else's mum. These days she was a teeny bit embarrassing...

It was partly the way she always wore such short skirts, and high heels.

It was partly the way she sang all the time at the top of her voice. And the way she did high kicks in public. And there was that awful bottom-wiggling thing she kept doing, too.

Worst of all, all Jessica's friends' dads fancied her mum rotten. And that was too embarrassing for words!

It was the end of term at Jessica's school. That was good news. To celebrate, the headteacher was holding a family fun day. There was going to be a concert, a dancing display and a chance for parents to meet the teachers. That was not such good news.

Jessica and her friends watched as the first few parents started arriving. A sports car purred up. Then an estate car. Then a brand new Land Rover. Jessica's school was a rather posh one, and the parents prided themselves on owning the most expensive cars.

Just then...

WHOP-WHOP-WHOP-WHOP-WHOP!

Everybody jumped as a purple helicopter roared past the window, dangerously low.

Jessica's cheeks turned pink, as people had a closer look. "It's Bee-Bee Bell!" the excited whispers went around.

Jessica rolled her eyes at her friends.

Sure enough, minutes later, there was
Bee-Bee Bell herself, clacking across the
school hall in sky-blue stilettoes. The sunlight
glittered on her silver spangly mini-dress.

CLACK

CLACK

"Jessica! Baby!"

Bee-Bee flung her arms around Jessica and kissed her cheeks twenty times, leaving a trail of purple lipstick prints. "Sweetie! I've missed you so much!" she cried dramatically.

Jessica tried to disentangle herself. "Mum! You only saw me at breakfast!"

Bee-Bee waved at all the other girls. "Hi kids. Love ya," she told them.

Then Bee-Bee pulled out a CD and brandished it in the air. "New album out next week, darlings. Don't forget!" She batted her eyelashes at some of the dads.

"Mum, stop it!" Jessica hissed, dragging her away to one side. "My classroom is this way. Come and see Miss Taylor."

Jessica led Bee-Bee to her classroom before her mum could say another thing.

As soon as Bee-Bee stepped into the room, Miss Taylor went all red and jittery. "Such a pleasure...allow me to take your coat, M-Ms Bell," she stuttered. "I'm such a huge fan!"

Bee-Bee tossed her hair. "New album out next week, doll," she said, with a ravishing smile. "Want an autograph?"

Jessica's mouth hung open. Surely nobody could call the strict Miss Taylor 'doll' and get away with it?

Miss Taylor was looking more starry-eyed than ever, though. "Y-Y-YES, please!" she stammered, scrabbling to find some paper. She pulled out an exercise book and ripped a page from it. "Here. This'll do."

"Hey!" Jessica said indignantly. "That's my English book!"

Neither Miss Taylor nor Bee-Bee were paying her any attention. As usual. Bee-Bee began reeling off a list of tour dates.

Jessica started to feel annoyed. She'd been hoping that Miss Taylor would tell her mum how well Jessica had been doing at science lately. Or mention that she'd been picked for the school choir.

"So, then we tour around Australia, before heading back for Christmas," Bee-Bee finished. She opened her handbag. "Here, have this," she said, pressing a pink fluffy pen into Miss Taylor's hand. "You can do your marking with it."

Jessica coughed loudly. "Talking of which...I came top in the maths test last week, didn't I, Miss Taylor?"

Miss Taylor didn't reply. She was gazing at the pen as if it was made of gold. "Oh, *thank you*, Ms Bell," she breathed.

Soon afterwards, it was time for the school concert. Once the parents were all seated, the whole school massed on stage to sing the school song.

FAMILY FUN DAY

The Swanky Hall Girls' School song had been written over a hundred years ago, and was rather a dirge.

Jessica stopped singing abruptly as she saw a familiar figure get to her feet in the audience. What was Bee-Bee doing?

The second verse of the school song had started but Jessica didn't join in. She was staring intently at her mum who was at the side of the stage, whispering to the headteacher. Jessica didn't like the look of this at all!

FUN DAY

"...*So lucky are we all*
To be pupils at Swanky Ha-a-a-all!"
As the song finished, there was a polite
round of applause from the parents. Then,
the headteacher came on stage.

"I've got a surprise for everybody," she beamed. "We have the brilliant Bee-Bee Bell with us today."

There was another round of applause. A couple of dads in the audience cheered. Bee-Bee waved a hand and gave a wiggle.

"And Miss Bell has very kindly offered to sing us her new single! Please put your hands together, everyone, for Bee-Bee Bell!"

Jessica tried not to groan out loud. Typical! Her mum couldn't even be near an audience without wanting to perform – even at her daughter's school!

Judging from the excited giggles and whispers on stage, nobody else seemed to mind. The girls all shuffled back to make room for Bee-Bee. Grabbing a microphone, she flicked her hair back, wiggled her bottom a few times and began to sing.

YOU LOOK LIKE AN ANGEL, SENT FROM HIGH ABOVE
OR ARE YOU JUST A DEVIL, TEASING WITH YOUR LOVE? ...
AY

The whole school was transfixed by the performance. Even Jessica had to admit that her mum's husky, honeyed tones sounded better than ever. The chorus was very catchy and by the end of the song, everyone was joining in and dancing.

CLAP

CLAP

Jessica winced as her mum did a few high kicks, and was given a huge round of applause. She was glad everyone had enjoyed the song, but she was even more glad it was over. Oh, why couldn't Mum be more like the other mums?

It was a relief when the concert ended.
After a picnic lunch and a dancing display,
it was finally time to go home.

Jessica couldn't wait. Having her own
mum take over the school concert was one
thing. But having her trying to join in the
dancing display had been more embarrassing
than anything!

Most people had
clapped at Bee-Bee's
twirls and wiggles.
But Jessica had heard
a couple of nasty
remarks, too.

"Who does she think
she is?" somebody
had said.

"Getting a bit old
for all of this now,
isn't she?" someone
else had muttered.

Jessica felt hot just
thinking about it.
Thank goodness they
were going home now!

As they walked towards the helicopter, Bee-Bee groaned, "These heels are evil, Jess!"

Jessica gave Bee-Bee a stern look. "You should wear your trainers, then," she said. "You don't *have* to get all dressed up to come to my school, you know."

Bee-Bee patted her arm. "That's what *you* think," she said. "First rule of showbiz, babe – if you want to be a superstar, you've gotta *look* like a superstar. All the time. Can't let the fans down, can I?" She glanced down at her outfit proudly.

"Well..." Jessica tried to think of the right words. "To be honest, Mum, all the parents there today came to see their daughters. Not you. So they weren't exactly fans."

Bee-Bee looked puzzled. "Yes, but..."

Jessica hadn't finished. "And your song
was lovely, but the concert was meant to be
a *school* concert – with just us girls singing."

Bee-Bee looked confused. "Yes, but..."

Jessica *still* hadn't finished. "And I know you're a good dancer, but so are the girls in Miss Ford's class – and they were the ones that everybody wanted to see!" She bit her lip. "Maybe next time, you could just *watch*, like all the other mums and dads?"

Bee-Bee tossed her head back. "But what about the second rule of showbiz?" she asked. "If you want to be a superstar, you've gotta *act* like a superstar. All the time!"

Jessica sighed. "Yes, but..." she said.

Bee-Bee hadn't finished. "Superstars do what they want! If I want to sing, I will. If I want to dance, I will." She looked around for inspiration. "And if I want to fly the helicopter home, then I will!"

Jessica turned pale. "No, Mum!" But Bee-Bee was already rushing ahead. Then she really did go flying – head over heels!

"No running, no dancing, and definitely no wiggling," the doctors said later, once they'd bandaged Bee-Bee. "For six weeks!"

"But I'm a superstar!" Bee-Bee wailed to Jessica. "This isn't supposed to happen!"

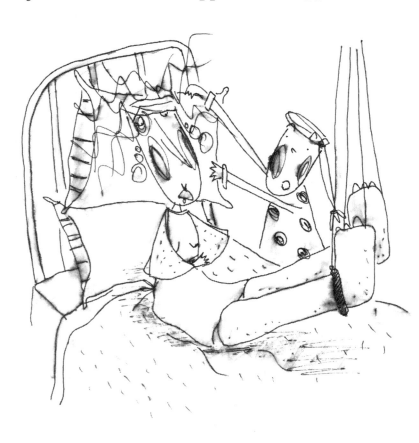

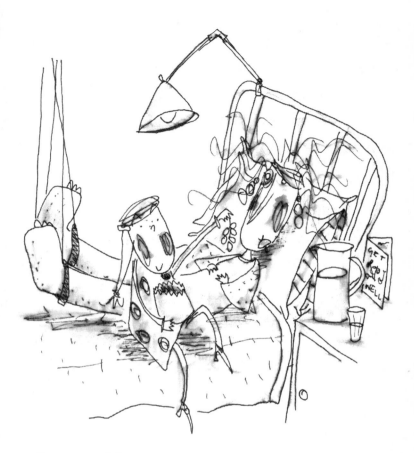

Bee-Bee blew her nose. "Now I can't even go on tour," she sighed.

Jessica passed her some grapes. "Don't worry, Mum," she said. "We'll still have a fun summer. Even superstars need a rest sometimes."

The rest of the summer was the calmest, most relaxing time of Jessica's whole life. Once Bee-Bee was home from hospital, she and Jessica spent their days eating grapes, playing battleships and reading.

When Bee-Bee felt up to it, Jessica wheeled her wheelchair to the ping-pong table and they had ping-pong tournaments.

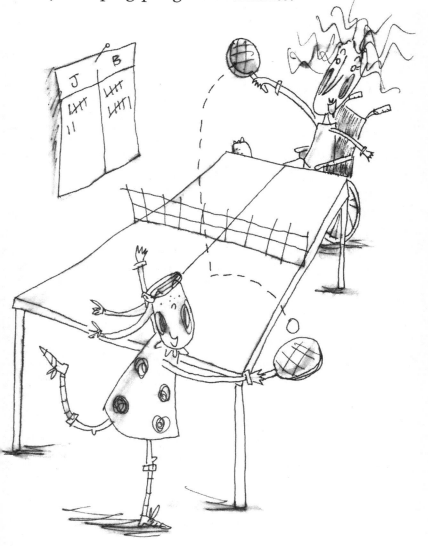

Sometimes they just watched funny videos all day and giggled like idiots.

And after a while, Bee-Bee realised that she was enjoying herself.

She had time to read all the celebrity magazines, and watch all the soap operas. She became an expert at ping-pong and battleships. And she was brilliant at catching grapes in her mouth. It was fantastic fun!

"Do you know what?" she said to Jessica after a particularly tense ping-pong match. "I'm not missing being a popstar at all. I've barely even thought about the new album or the cancelled world tour. I'm far too hooked on my soap operas to miss them now!"

Jessica looked over at her mum, sitting up in bed with no make-up, scruffy hair and her favourite slippers on. She didn't even *look* like a popstar these days. She looked just like a normal mum. It was brilliant.

"I don't miss popstar Bee-Bee either," Jessica smiled. "I like you much more when you're just Mum."

Once Bee-Bee was out of her wheelchair, Jessica was half-expecting her mum to go back to her old popstar ways. But Bee-Bee seemed a changed woman. She took up gardening.

She joined the local ping-pong club.

She even gave an enormous pile of spangly
mini-dresses to charity.

"I'm retiring," she announced to the press.
"I'm having far too much fun to get back
into the studio. Life's too short to be
a popstar all the time!" Jessica could
hardly believe it.

But then, on the last day of the summer
holidays, Jessica was woken up by the noise
of a minibus beeping.

"Come in, come in!" she heard her
mum calling.

Jessica peeped out of her bedroom window.
There was her mum on the front steps, still
on crutches, in a bright pink mini-dress, full
make-up and the highest heels Jessica had
ever seen.

Jessica rubbed her eyes, hoping she was just half-asleep and imagining things. But Bee-Bee was still there, looking as much a pop diva as ever.

Jessica opened her window. "Mum!" she called. "What's going on?"

Bee-Bee was beckoning in a group of people all clutching ping-pong bats and looking awestruck. She grinned up at Jessica. "Ping-Pong All-Day Tournament. Come and join us if you want."

Jessica started to laugh. Ping-Pong All-Day Tournament? Surely her mum was the only woman in the world who would dress up in a pink mini-dress for that!

"Well, Mum," she said. "You know what the third rule of showbiz is. If you want to be a superstar – *play ping-pong* like a superstar!" Bee-Bee winked. "Exactly," she said.

Jessica laughed even harder. Mum was never going to change that much, was she? She was always going to be a superstar at heart.

Jessica winked back at Bee-Bee. "Go get
'em, Mum," she said. "With a dress like that,
how can you possibly lose?"

FRIGHTFUL FAMILIES

WRITTEN BY SUE MONGREDIEN • ILLUSTRATED BY TERESA MURFI

Explorer Trauma	1 84362 563 6
Headmaster Disaster	1 84362 564 4
Millionaire Mayhem	1 84362 565 2
Clown Calamity	1 84362 566 0
Popstar Panic	1 84362 567 9
Football-mad Dad	1 84362 568 7
Chef Shocker	1 84362 569 5
Astronerds	1 84362 570 9

All priced at £8.99

Frightful Families are available from all good bookshops, or can be ordered direct from the publisher: Orchard Books, PO BOX 29, Douglas IM99 1BQ
Credit card orders please telephone 01624 836000
or fax 01624 837033 or visit our Internet site: www.wattspub.co.uk
or e-mail: bookshop@enterprise.net for details.

To order please quote title, author and ISBN
and your full name and address.
Cheques and postal orders should be made payable to 'Bookpost plc.'
Postage and packing is FREE within the UK
(overseas customers should add £1.00 per book).
Prices and availability are subject to change.